This book
belongs to

_____

_____

The
Sleepy
Teddy Bear

AND OTHER TOYBOX STORIES

The Sleepy Teddy Bear

AND OTHER TOYBOX STORIES

P
PARRAGON

First published in Great Britain in 1998 by
Parragon
13 Whiteladies Road
Clifton
Bristol BS8 1PB

Copyright © Parragon 1998

ISBN 0 75252-528-X

Printed in Great Britain

Reprinted in 1999

Produced by Nicola Baxter
PO Box 71
Diss Norfolk IP22 2DT

Stories by Nicola Baxter, except
Daisy, the Runaway Doll by Ronne Randall
Designed by Amanda Hawkes
Text illustrations by Duncan Gutteridge
Cover illustration by Alisa Tingley

Contents

The Sleepy Teddy Bear

Adam had a beautiful teddy bear called Mr Muffle. He had lovely golden fur and two bright little eyes. Adam's grandmother thought he looked a little chilly one winter's day, so she knitted him a bright red sweater. Adam felt that he was a very special teddy bear indeed.

Mr Muffle had lots of jobs to do. He kept an eye on things in Adam's room during the day, when Adam was out and about. He warmed up Adam's bed in the evening, ready for him to jump into after his bath. And *just* before Adam got into bed, Mr Muffle had his most important task of all. He had to check under the bed for *monsters*. Adam had once read a story about a monster who lived under a little boy's bed. The more he read about it, the more likely it seemed to him that the fluffy, dark space under his bed was just the kind of place that a monster might love to live. And you never knew when a monster might move in. That was why Mr Muffles had to look under the bed *every* night.

When Mr Muffles had checked very carefully under the bed (and had a quick look behind the curtains as well, just to be on the safe side), Adam was happy to cuddle down between the sheets and go to sleep. He didn't need his bedroom door to be a ajar or a night light on his bedside table. He knew that he was as safe as he could be with Mr Muffles beside him.

One evening in late autumn, when it was already dark outside, Adam's mother looked at the clock and told him it was time for his bath and bed. Adam was in the middle of playing with his new space game, so he pretended not to hear her.

"Adam!" called his mother. "I know you can hear me, even on

Mars. Put your toys away now and get ready for bed. We're already quite late this evening."

"All right, Mum," said Adam, reluctantly. He really didn't feel like going to bed yet. As he was putting the pieces of his space game back in the box, one of them rolled under the table, and Adam gave it another nudge with his foot.

"Mum," he said, "I can't go yet. I've lost one of the pieces of my game. I must find it before I go to bed or … or … I won't be able to sleep because I'll be worried."

"All right," sighed Adam's mother, and she got down on her

hands and knees to help him look for the missing piece.

It took quite a long time to find the piece under the table, partly because Adam managed to "search" between his mother and the table most of the time, but at last it was found.

"Now hurry up!" said Mum. "It's an hour past your bedtime. Just a quick bath, Adam, and no more delays please."

Adam felt a little bit guilty as he scampered up the stairs. He thought for a moment about "losing" one of the ducks from his bath, but he was beginning to be quite tired now.

The sleepy boy had his bath in double-quick time. I'm pretty sure that there were lots of parts of him that were not much cleaner after his bath than they were before it. (Adam never was very keen on washing his *ears*, for example!)

When Adam went into his bedroom, he knew at once that something was different. In fact, something was more than different – it was *wrong*! It took him a moment to realise what the problem was.

Mr Muffles was asleep! Yes, the teddy bear in the red sweater was sitting in his usual place on the bed, but there was no doubt about it, those bright little beady eyes were closed. A tiny snoring sound came from Mr Muffles' furry chest.

Adam climbed into bed and clutched Mr Muffles, who did not wake up.

"Goodnight!" said Adam's mother from the doorway. "Go straight to sleep now! And goodnight, Mr Muffles!"

"But Mum!" called Adam. "Mr Muffles is already asleep!"

"I'm not surprised," said his mother. "Have you seen what the time is? All boys and their bears should be fast asleep by now. Goodnight!"

Well, Adam settled down into his bed. He felt more sleepy than ever, but every time he closed his eyes, a worrying thought would pop into his mind. Mr Muffles hadn't checked under the bed. What if there was something green and hairy under there, just waiting until he was asleep? Or, worse still, what if there was something purple and slimy under there, ready to ooze across the carpet as soon as the coast was clear? Or what about something brown and prickly, with very sharp teeth?

Adam could feel a tingling at the tips of his toes, just where a monster might decide to nibble first on its midnight snack.

Adam gave Mr Muffles a little shake. "Wake up!" he whispered. "Mr Muffles! Wake up!" But the silly old teddy bear just carried on sleeping.

Adam tried very hard to be sensible. "There was no monster under the bed last night," he said to himself, "and no monster the

night before that, *or* the night
before that. In fact, there has
never been a monster under the
bed, so there won't be one now."

Still, at the back of his mind, a
little voice was saying, "You
don't *know* that there isn't a
monster tonight, because
nobody has checked to see. And
it *would* be the very night that
nobody checked when a monster
might come."

Adam lay awake in the
darkness and listened very
carefully. He was almost sure he
could hear a sort of scrabbling,
scratching, snorting sound
coming from you-know-where.

And wasn't that a slobbering, squelching, sucking kind of noise, coming from somewhere down by his toes?

Adam decided to be brave. He switched on the bedside light and got out of bed. If Mr Muffles had the courage to look under the bed, then so did he.

First Adam rummaged in his chest of drawers for his torch. It was true that Mr Muffles didn't use a torch, but then bear eyes are much sharper than human ones, as everyone knows.

Adam found his torch and turned it on. He knelt down very quietly and took a deep breath.

What was best? To snatch up the corner of the quilt and have one quick look? Or to lift the quilt gently, gently and very slowly peep under the bed? Adam couldn't make up his mind. Mr Muffles did one quick look, but then he was used to the job. Adam felt that a beginner should perhaps move more slowly – to make sure he did the job thoroughly, of course.

So very, very slowly, Adam bent down, and very, very gently, he lifted up the corner of his quilt. Bending closer, he peered into the space under the bed, into the dusty dark.

"Aaaaaaaagh!" yelled Adam, as he realised what he was seeing.

"Aaaaaaaagh!" yelled the monster, blinking its yellow eyes.

Yes, there *was* a monster under the bed, and it looked just as frightened as Adam was!

Now all the time that Adam had been getting ready to look under the bed, he had only half believed there might be a monster. If you had asked him to say whether, in his heart of hearts, he really thought there was a monster under his bed, then he would have said, "No, of course not. No one *really* has monsters *anywhere*."

But here he was, face to face with a monster. Adam rubbed his eyes. The easiest reason for seeing a monster might be that he was already asleep. But Adam was awake all right. He was particularly sure after he had rubbed his eyes, because he had forgotten that he was still holding the torch and he managed to clonk himself on the forehead with it.

"Oooooh!" said the monster, sympathetically.

Adam smiled. It was really quite a friendly looking monster, even if it did have green spots and funny purple hair.

The monster smiled. He had a lot of rather sharp-looking little teeth, but then so do kittens, and everyone thinks *they* are cute.

"I'm a monster," said the monster, "in case you didn't realise." He had quite a high-pitched, squeaky little voice.

"I'm Adam," said Adam. "I'm a boy," he added, in case the monster wasn't very used to humans. "Er ... have you lived here long?"

"Oh, a few months now," said the monster carelessly. "It's a very nice bed to live under. The last one I had was always being swept and cleaned. You know,

there is nothing in the world that
monsters hate more than
vacuum cleaners. Ugh!"

"What else is under there?"
asked Adam curiously, peering
past the monster.

"Well, now, this is my private
place, so I think that's *my*
business," said the monster,
primly. "But if you're thinking
about that football sock you lost,
yes, it is here, and no, you can't
have it back."

"All right," said Adam. "I've got
some new ones now, anyway."

Adam tried to think what his
next question should be, but
really he had so many, he hardly

knew where to begin. Then he thought of something that was really quite important. The trouble was, it was quite a delicate matter, too.

"I was wondering," said Adam, "whether you have everything you need under there. You know, food and so on?"

"You want to know if I'm going to eat you," said the monster, with a nasty little giggle but a rather nice smile.

"Well, I did wonder," said Adam, trying to look as if he didn't mind very much one way or the other. "What *do* monsters eat these days?"

The monster giggled again. "Don't worry," he said, "I survive very nicely on the odd spider that crawls down the corner. Delicious!"

Adam felt a little better after that, but it didn't seem right, somehow, just to get back into bed and go to sleep. He wondered if he really would be able to sleep, *knowing* that there was a monster under the bed, however friendly it was.

Just then, Adam heard a little snuffling sound. It was Mr Muffles, waking up at last! With a soft thud, Mr Muffles landed on the floor beside Adam.

The sleepy teddy bear took in the situation at a glance.

"Ah," he said, "I see that you two have met."

Adam felt strongly that Mr Muffles had some explaining to do. After all, he had been failing in his most important job.

"Night after night, Mr Muffles," said Adam, "you promised me that there were no monsters under my bed. And yet you knew that there was at least one! How do you explain that?"

"Now, Adam," said Mr Muffles, trying to sound like an old and wise bear, "I never actually said that there were no monsters. *You* said, 'Is everything all right under the bed?' and I said, 'Yes!' As you can see, it was all right. It's just that there is a little tiny monster there as well."

"But how did you know it was all right?" asked Adam. "How did you know he wasn't a really very dangerous monster, who might crunch teddy bears and leave only their ears on the pillow in the morning?"

"*Please*, said Mr Muffles, "do give me credit for some sense. The monster and I have had some long chats while you were asleep. I was quite sure that no harm would come to us."

"And what do we do now?" asked Adam. "That's what I'd like to know."

"I can quite see," said Mr Muffles, "that from your point of view things are rather different now. Sleeping with a monster under the bed that you don't know is there is a very different matter from sleeping with a monster under the bed that you *do* know is there. Do you think you could ever get used to the idea, Adam?"

"I don't think so," said Adam. "It doesn't feel right, somehow."

"Very well," said Mr Muffles, then I have another idea.

If you were to creep into Adam's room tonight, you would see a very strange sight. Adam and the monster sleep *in* the bed, and Adam finds that the monster is every bit as cuddly as Mr Muffles. The teddy bear sleeps *under* the bed, so that he can make sure that no new monsters try to take over the space during the night. During the day, they swap over.

So remember, a monster under the bed is not the end of the world, but do make sure your teddy bear is doing his job properly each night, won't you?

Daisy, the Runaway Doll

Daisy fancied herself the smartest, the most beautiful, the best dressed, and altogether the most elegant of all the dolls in Laura's room.

For one thing, although everyone called her Daisy, her full name was much grander. It was Daisy Dorinda Deborah Delilah Dinah Darlington Dean. For another thing, there was only one of her – not like some other dolls, who have identical sisters or brothers everywhere you care to look!

No, Daisy was very, very special. She had been handmade by Laura's Aunt Susan, who had given her to Laura for her fourth birthday. Her eyes were made of shiny black buttons. Her hair was made of the finest sunflower-gold wool. Her smile was sewn on with rosy red thread. She had three beautiful dresses, all with matching shoes and lacy socks. She had her own suitcase for all her finery and her own little blue umbrella. She sat proudly in her own special place on Laura's bed.

Laura took good care of Daisy. Every day she combed her golden hair, dressed her up in one of her beautiful dresses, and took her out in her buggy. Laura took Daisy to the park, to the shops, and to visit friends. Sometimes Laura had tea parties, and Daisy was always the guest of honour. Laura loved Daisy, and Daisy loved Laura, and they were happy together.

Things went on in this pleasant, carefree way for a long time. Then, one summer afternoon, something terrible happened.

A *dog* came to live with Laura and her parents. He was a big, sloppy, floppy-eared, tail-wagging, hairy, muddy-pawed spaniel called Max. And Laura loved *him*, just as she loved Daisy.

It wouldn't have been so bad if Max had stayed out in the garden.

But to Daisy's dismay, he was allowed in the house with Laura and her mother and father. Max was even allowed in Laura's room! And, to Daisy's horror, he was sometimes even allowed to jump up on the bed! Then he would snuffle and nuzzle Daisy with his big wet nose, until Laura called him away.

"Come on, Max," Laura would say happily. "Catch the ball!" And she would grab her blue rubber ball and throw it into the air. Max, his ears flying and his tail flapping wildly, would leap into the air and catch the ball in his big, wet mouth. Then he would bound across the room, set the ball at Laura's feet, and wait for her to do it all again.

Max never watched where he was going, and he didn't care who or what was in the way. He often stepped on Laura's cuddly toys with his big clumsy paws. He knocked down her trucks and cars and books with his wagging tail. He crashed into the house where the little tiny dolls lived and knocked it over. And sometimes he picked up Laura's teddy bear and flung him right into the air!

The amazing thing was that neither Laura nor any of the

other toys seemed to mind all this madness and mayhem. In fact, they all seemed to *enjoy* playing with Max! But Daisy didn't want any part of his rowdy games, and she always shrank back when she heard Max's bark.

But the more she shrank back, the more Max seemed to want to play with her. "Come on!" he would yap at Daisy. "Please play with me! I'll give you a ride in the air! Old Teddy loves it, and you might too!"

"Go away, you monster!" Daisy would hiss at Max when Laura's back was turned. "Leave me alone! Just leave me alone!"

One morning towards the end of summer, Laura got dressed in some smart new clothes.

"I'm starting school today," she told Daisy, "so I won't be able to play with you so much. But don't worry. Max will look after you, won't you, Max?"

Right behind her, Max wagged his tail enthusiastically.

Later, when Daisy heard the door close behind Laura and her Mum, she dreaded what would happen next. Any minute now…

"*Woof! Woof!* Who's ready for some fun?" barked Max, as he came hurtling into the room with his floppy ears flying.

"I am! I am!" shouted Old Teddy. "I want to go flying high in the air!"

"We are! We are!" squealed the little tiny dolls. "Let's play 'Earthquake' again, Max, where you rattle the dolls' house and make everything wobbly!"

"I'm ready, Max!" called Cuddly Bunny. "Play 'Elephant Steps' on my tummy, Max!"

But Max knew who *he* wanted to play with. He leapt up on to the bed and bounded towards Daisy, the dainty doll.

"Come on, Daisy," he barked, tugging at her arm. "You'll have fun, really!"

"Leave me alone!" snapped Daisy. "Go away, before you mess up my golden hair and tear my beautiful clothes!"

"I'll be careful," barked Max eagerly. "I promise!"

"No," said Daisy, "no, no, NO!"

So Max went off to play with the other toys until Laura came home again.

The same thing happened the next day, and the next. Each morning, Max would jump up on the bed and say, "Will you play with me today, Daisy?" And each day, Daisy's answer was exactly the same.

"No, no, no. And that is *final*!"

But Max just would not give up, and after several weeks of this, one morning he went too far. He tugged and tugged at Daisy's arm until he pulled the sleeve of her beautiful dress right off!

"Now look what you've done!" shouted Daisy. "That does it. I'm leaving. I have to go away and find another home – one without a *dog*!"

And with that, Daisy climbed down from the bed, packed all her things in her carrying case, and ran out of the room. A moment later, she was *thumpety-thumpety-thumpeting* down the stairs, trailing her case and her own special blue umbrella behind her.

"Daisy, wait!" called Max. "What will Laura say?"

"Come back, Daisy! Come back!" cried Old Teddy, Cuddly Bunny and the little tiny dolls.

But Daisy was not turning back. She ran into the living room, clambered up on to the sofa, and went right out through the open window. A second later, she was in the flowerbed in the front garden.

It had rained the night before, and the flowerbed was muddy and damp. As Daisy stood up, she realised that her blue dress was a bit stained and soggy.

"Never mind," she thought. "I have to keep going. I'll be all right once I've found a lovely new home."

Daisy had never been out on her own before, but she had been out with Laura dozens and dozens of times. She knew the way to Laura's friend Katie's house. She knew the way to the shops. And she knew the way to the park.

So Daisy picked up her case and her umbrella and began making her way down the garden. *Squelch, squelch, squelch, splotch* went her smart shoes in the mud. Her lacy white socks were soon soaked through, and she began to feel cold, but she made herself keep going.

By the time Daisy reached the pavement, it was nearly midday. She was exhausted. It is one thing to be pushed somewhere in a buggy, but quite another to have to walk there on your own

little legs. No wonder the poor
doll was tired! But Daisy knew
she had a long way to go, and she
wanted to get to the park before
nightfall, so she didn't stop.

As Daisy started her journey
down the pavement, the wind
began to blow and the sky grew
grey. Moments later, big heavy
raindrops plopped down on to
Daisy. She struggled to put up
her little blue umbrella, but it
was so tiny that the big drops of
rain simply splashed over the
edge and into her face. Soon her
clothes and her hair were
soaked. In fact, Daisy's whole
self, right through to her insides,

was drenched and cold. She was shivering terribly and felt faint.

"It's no use," Daisy said to herself. "I'll have to stop and rest, just for a bit. There are some leaves under those big trees ... they'll be soft to lie on ... I'll just rest for a little while ... just a little while..." Wearily,

Daisy collapsed on to the small pile of leaves. Her button eyes closed, and she fell fast asleep. All the while, the rain kept falling, and the wind kept blowing, colder and colder.

Hours later, Daisy woke with a start. The rain had stopped, but darkness surrounded the dainty doll. When she tried to move, she found she couldn't. She was trapped in a great heap of cold, wet leaves. In the tree above her, an owl hooted eerily and flapped its wings. The sound made the poor doll even more frightened. She was alone in a strange place, with no one to help her.

"Oh, what will happen to me now?" Daisy thought, trembling with cold and fear. Remembering Laura's soft, warm bed – and Laura's soft, warm arms around her – she began to cry.

"Why did I ever run away?" she sobbed. "How I wish I were back home, safe with Laura!"

As she lay there in the leaves, weeping and wishing, Daisy

suddenly heard something – a sound she knew well. It was a bark, an excited, happy bark, and it sounded so sweet to Daisy.

"Max!" cried Daisy. "Max! Help!" But she needn't have bothered calling. Max knew just where she was, and he was galloping towards her. A moment later, she heard the familiar snuffle and felt Max's cold, wet nose nudging its way through the leaves. Then, ever so gently, Max grabbed hold of Daisy with his mouth and pulled her out.

"Oh, Max, you found Daisy!" cried Laura, running towards them. "Look, Mum!" she called.

"Here she is! Oh, I can't believe it! Max found Daisy!"

When Laura took her and held her tight, Daisy felt happier than she ever had before.

"Let's have a look," said Laura's Mum, crouching down. "Hmm … I think after a wash in some warm, soapy water and a little work with a needle and thread, Daisy should look as beautiful as ever."

"It doesn't matter what she *looks* like, Mum," said Laura. "The important thing is that she's back – and Max found her! You're a very clever dog, Max! You're a very clever dog indeed!"

As Laura reached down to give Max a pat on the head, Daisy looked down at him, too. Max was the only one who noticed that at that moment, Daisy's smile grew just a little wider, and one of her shiny button eyes winked. It was a wink that said, "I think you're clever too – friend!"

The
Toy Train

In the nursery class, there were lots of toys for children to play with. The little ones came every day for two hours in the morning and two hours in the afternoon. They did painting – and painted their faces as well as their pictures. They did modelling – and had to be stopped from eating half the clay. They did dancing – and sometimes kicked each other only half by mistake. They did singing – and sometimes you could recognise the tune!

In the afternoon, the children had a quiet time, when the teacher read them a story. They had a mug of juice or milk and some fruit, and some of them had a little sleep afterwards as well. Then it was time to play with the toys. And this time frightened some of the toys very much indeed.

"It isn't that they mean to be rough," said the ragdoll, one evening after the children had gone home. "That little boy with the curly hair wanted to play doctors, and he decided to chop my leg off! It was lucky the teacher noticed in time!"

The other toys shuddered at this dreadful story.

"It was the same for me," said the rocking horse, shaking her silky mane. "If only the teacher hadn't read a story about zebras to those silly children, they would never have tried to paint purple stripes on me!"

"Just think yourself lucky you don't have wheels," grumbled the truck. "I can't remember the last time I had a full set of four wheels. If one of them is found, another is lost, and I know that one of them is under the toy cupboard, where it will *never* be found. And don't talk to me about my suspension! It's no fun driving on your axles, I can tell you. No fun at all."

"You're right there," agreed the tractor, "and it's no fun being driven into walls and doors and people's legs either. And when a child bursts into tears, it's never their fault, you notice. Everyone complains that there are sharp bits on the toys. They say we're dangerous and should be … I can hardly say it … thrown away. I wouldn't have sharp bits if I hadn't been bashed into a wall over and over again!"

Now it happened about this time that a kind aunty gave the

nursery class a brand new train
for the children to play with. It
had a shiny red funnel and bright
blue paintwork. Its wheels were
black, and its carriages were
yellow. It even still had its own
cardboard box!

The train had overheard the toys' complaints. "That kind of thing won't happen to me," it said to itself. "When they see how shiny and new I am, the children will be really careful with me."

The next day, the train was taken down from its shelf and given to a little girl to play with. She pushed it along quite happily for a while, but then she decided it needed some goods in its carriages. She put some modelling clay in the first one. She poured some paint in the second one. In the third carriage, she put half a sandwich left over from her lunch (and she had to squidge it a bit to make it fit). Then she had a wonderful time making the train crash into the long-suffering tractor.

By the time the children had put their coats on to go home, the train did not look like a new toy any more. Its paint was scratched and its funnel was bent. At least one of the teachers cleaned out its carriages and pushed the funnel back into shape before she went home.

That night, the toys grumbled as usual, and this time the train knew exactly what they were talking about.

"I'm not going to stay here with this kind of treatment," it said. "I'm off!" And to the amazement of the other toys, the train whizzed along the shelf and zoomed out of the top of the window, which happened to be open just far enough.

Crash! The train landed with a bump on the grass below, but all its carriages were still connected, so it felt ready for an adventure. The moon and stars were shining, as it set off to find a new home.

All that night, the little train whizzed along. At first it was travelling along pavements, but soon it came into the real countryside, where there were only roads with grass beside them. The little train soon found that it was not safe to chuff along on the roads. The puffing vehicle was too small for cars and trucks to see. One van almost squashed it, and another threw water from a puddle all over it. After that, the little train whizzed into a gateway and set off across a field.

It is not easy for trains to travel through tall grass and flowers, but as the sun rose, the

little train felt quite cheerful. At least it was not about to be bashed or stuffed with stale sandwiches! All it needed to do was to find a new place to live, where it would be treated with some respect.

As luck would have it, the little train soon puffed into the garden of a large house. It was quite astonished to see another train whizzing towards it, travelling on a track laid all the way round the garden. The other train did not seem to want to stop to talk but zoomed past, blowing its whistle. The little train at once hopped on to the tracks and set off after it.

How much easier it was to travel on tracks! The little train enjoyed itself as it chuffed along. It was just giving a little *toot! toot!* as it went round a bend, when a large hand reached down and picked it up.

"Whatever is this?" asked a deep voice. It was the man who owned the house. He was a model-train collector, amazed to see a strange train chuffing round his tracks. "One of my friends must have put it here as a surprise," he said to himself. "Hmmm, it's not in very good condition. I must do some work on this one."

The train could hardly believe its luck. It soon found itself in the collector's workshop, where its scratches were painted and its funnel was made properly straight again.

By the time the man had finished, the train looked as good as new – better than new, in fact, because it had been given a special polish that made it glisten and gleam.

Proudly, the man placed the train in a special cabinet, with a light above it so that everyone one could see how beautiful it looked. He wrote a little label and put it beside the train.

"I've really fallen on my wheels here," thought the train. "There could be no better place for a toy train to live."

It was true that the train never had to worry about being scratched and bashed. The man had so many different trains that he did not often take the little train from its cabinet. Day after day, the little train sat there, looking perfect. There was not a speck of dust on its carriages or a smudge on its paintwork. It looked wonderful – and it *felt* very unhappy.

Isn't that train ever satisfied? you will ask. Sometimes it takes all of us a long time to find out what we really need. As it sat on its special shelf, the little train began to understand what all toys learn in the end: toys are meant to be played with, and they are not happy without children to love them – yes, and bash them and scratch them and squidge sandwiches into them sometimes as well.

It was several months before the little train had a chance to escape. Then, one evening, the collector took it into the garden for a whiz around the tracks. At the bottom of the garden, behind some bushes, the little train

whizzed right off those tracks
and off into the countryside.

It would be too much to expect
that the little train found its way
back to the nursery where it
began, but it did find the house
of a little girl and boy who were
just delighted to have a new toy
to play with. I would like to be
able to tell you that they looked
after the little train and were
careful with it, but that wouldn't

be true. They bashed it, they scratched it and they squidged not only sandwiches but several doughnuts and half a chocolate sponge cake into its carriages as well. Yes, they really loved their beautiful train.

And the little train? It has the kind of smile on his face that only a very bashed, scratched and squidged train can have. And, you know, it is as happy as a train can be.

The
Lonely
Panda

Pamela Panda belonged to a little boy called Jack. He played with her a lot when he was small, but now that he was a much bigger boy, he preferred his trucks and his little kitchen and his farm.

Toys expect that kind of thing. They know that children grow up and pass on to other kinds of amusements. It is a little bit sad, but very often the old toys are able to play together (when human beings are not looking, of course), so they have a happy life. Later, if they are lucky, they may be given to another little boy or girl, who will love and care for them just as well as the first one did.

Pamela Panda was a beautiful fluffy black and white bear. She had been given to Jack when he was a baby, and he loved to chew her black ears and lay his little head on her white tummy. Several times during those early years, Pamela had got dirty and messy, but she was a very *washable* bear, so when Jack's Mum had given her a twirl in the washing machine, she came out looking like new.

The unfortunate thing was that Pamela was such a favourite with Jack in the early days that the other toys didn't get much of a chance to play with the little boy.

"It's not fair," grumbled the twin teddy bears. "He plays with that panda all the time, and she's no better than we are."

"She thinks she's superior to the rest of us," said the toy train. "You can tell by the way she points her nose in the air. I don't think she's very friendly."

In fact, Pamela Panda pointed her nose just the way it had been made back in China, and the toys knew that really, but they were upset that they were hardly ever chosen as playthings, so they pretended not to like her.

As time went on, the toys forgot that they really didn't know anything about Pamela. The stories they had made up about her being cold and stand-offish were told over and over again, until everyone simply assumed that they were true. So none of the other toys talked to the panda at all.

Pamela was hurt by the other toys' attitude, but she didn't mind too much while Jack was her best friend. And perhaps she didn't try quite as hard as she might have done to be friendly, knowing that she always had Jack to play with.

"You see, we were right," the twin teddies would say. "She *is* unfriendly, just as we said. Well, if that's the way she wants it…"

Very gradually, Jack grew up. Soon he was crawling around the room and pulling himself up on the furniture. He did still play with Pamela, but he didn't chew her ears or stroke her tummy any more. No, now he picked her up and whirled her round his head by the arm, before throwing her as far as he could across the room.

"Ouch!" Pamela Panda was glad of her soft fur to cushion her landing. She really preferred *not* to be thrown around like that, but it was better than not being played with at all.

Very soon, Jack took his first wobbly steps. Pamela watched with pride, convinced that she had helped him to grow so big and strong. She would have liked to have shared her pride with the other toys, but when she turned to them, they shrugged their shoulders and looked away.

As soon as Jack was toddling about the room, he lost interest in Pamela. Oh, sometimes he jumped up and down on her, and for a little while he still liked to have her in his bed at night, but more and more now she was simply left on the shelf. Poor Pamela felt very lonely. Perhaps now the other toys would be more friendly.

But during the day, the dolls and bears talked to each other, chattering so hard that there was no room for an outsider to make herself heard.

At night, the other toys cuddled up together, and the twin teddy bears had their own little cushion, where they slept next to each other. Poor Pamela didn't know whether the days or the nights were worse. She felt sad *all* the time.

About this time, Jack started
to be very interested in books.
He would sit with his Mum,
turning the thick cardboard
pages and looking at all the
colourful pictures.

"Look, darling," his Mum would say, pointing to a picture of a truck, "that's just like your truck. And there are some red boots, just like yours. What else can you see on this page?"

Jack would point to a picture of a teddy bear and a train and try to say the words.

"And look here," his Mum would say. "Here's a picture of a panda. Do you think it's a friend of Pamela's?"

But Jack was bored now and slipped off her lap to play with his farm animals.

Jack's Mum put the book down on a table, and as soon as her

back was turned, Pamela slipped across and took a look at it. Yes, there was a picture of a panda, and it looked just like her! It had black ears and a white tummy, and it looked so friendly and cuddly. Pamela gave a big sigh. Why couldn't she have a twin like the teddy bears? It would be so lovely to have a friend to play with, especially a friend who was just like her!

Then Pamela had an idea. She had to wait until no one was around. Then she climbed up on to Jack's little stool and stood up. If she stood on the very tips of her paws, she could just reach to jump on to the dressing table, where Jack's Mum had put a large mirror.

Pamela raised her eyes slowly to the glass. There was another panda, just a pretty as she was, and it was smiling right at her!

"Hello!" said Pamela.

"Hello!" said the other panda.

Soon Pamela found that she could have lovely chats with the new panda. At the back of her mind, of course, she knew that she was talking to her own reflection, but she wanted so much to have a friend of her own that most of the time she didn't think about that.

The other toys simply didn't understand what she was doing.

"Just look at her," said the toy train. "She's so vain and stuck up she only ever wants to talk to herself. She's too good for us – at least, that's what *she* thinks!"

Things might have gone on in this unhappy way if Jack's cousin Joshua had not come to stay. Joshua was a year or so older than Jack and he was a *terror*!

Only two hours after Joshua's arrival, the toys were trembling in their shoes. He had stamped on the toy train. He had pulled the arms off the parachuting doll. He had made a little hole in the toy duck to see what his stuffing was made of. But worse was to follow.

That afternoon, Jack and his cousin went outside looking for adventures. They took with them some of the toys from Jack's room as part of the expedition team.

"We might want some of them to go first into dangerous places, to make sure it is safe," said Joshua wisely.

The toys shuddered as they were pulled along in the trolley that usually held Jack's bricks.

"What do you think they are going to do with us?" whispered the twin teddy bears.

"Sshhh!" said the toy duck. "I've suffered enough already. I want them to forget I'm here."

Soon the boys reached the ditch at the end of the garden.

"We're not allowed to go across," said Jack. "Mum won't let me."

"No, but we could throw these toys across," said Joshua, "and see which ones can reach the other side."

Jack wasn't sure at first, but he was quite keen to show off his throwing, which, as we know, was pretty good.

"All right," he said. "I'll go first!" And he picked up one of

the twin teddy bears and threw it
as far as he could, right over to
the other side of the ditch.

The boys had a lovely time,
before long both the bears, and
the toy duck, and Pamela Panda
were lying in a heap on the other
side of the ditch. Then Jack and
Joshua went off to have their
lunch and forgot all about the
rest of their expedition.

Out in the cold field, the toys
were moaning and groaning.

"We'll never be found here on
the ploughed earth. It's just the
same colour as our fur," said one
of the teddy bears. "We'll have to
stay here all summer. Then the

farmer will plough us up and that will be the end of us!"

But Pamela Panda was busy wriggling and jiggling on the bottom of the pile.

"Just let me get to the top," she puffed.

"Oh, that's typical," said the toy duck. "Why should you be on top of the pile, that's what I'd like to know?"

"Because," said Pamela, "I'm black and white. I'm the one that Jack's Mum will be able to see from far away when she comes to look for us this afternoon."

The toys were silent for a moment. What Pamela had said

was certainly very sensible. They let her wriggle her way to the very top.

"Now," said Pamela, "it may be a long time before we are rescued, so I suggest we sing some songs and tell jokes. It will keep our spirits up."

The toys could hardly believe their ears. Was this the stuck-up panda who preferred her own company to theirs?

That afternoon, as they all lay together in the field, the toys learnt a lot more about Pamela, and she learnt a lot more about *them*. But one of the teddy bears was still not sure.

"What I don't understand," he said, "is why you spend so much time looking in the mirror. You're a fine looking panda, I know, but even so, it looks rather vain."

Then Pamela explained that she had been so lonely, she had talked to her own reflection sometimes, pretending it was another panda.

The toys were silent for a moment. Then they all spoke at once and from their hearts.

"We're sorry," they said. "Let's all be friends now, shall we?"

"Oh yes," agreed Pamela. "And here comes Jack's Mum. We'll soon be safe and sound."

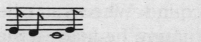

The
Singing
Bear

Once upon a time, there was a teddy bear with a beautiful voice. When you shook him gently, he made a deep, growling sound. When you poked his tummy, he made a friendly, humming sound. And when you patted him firmly on the back, he said quite distinctly, "Hello! I'm Bernard Bear!"

As you can imagine, Bernard Bear was a great favourite in the nursery. All the children loved to play with him, and best of all they liked to make him talk. In fact, if you shook, poked and patted Bernard in the right way, you could have quite a long conversation with him. It was lovely for the little ones.

But Bernard Bear was not content with the sounds he could make. He thought that he could do better. One day, a little girl brought a musical box to the nursery. When you opened the lid, a little dancer inside twirled round and round, and music played. It was quite soft and tinkling, but everyone could hear that the musical box played "Twinkle, twinkle, little star."

Bernard Bear was most impressed by the box. "If a silly thing like that can sing a tune, then surely a clever bear like me can do it," he said to himself. "It's time I started to practise."

Bernard Bear was determined to sing at all costs. He took a deep breath and opened his mouth. "Grrrrr," he said. "Grrrrr. Grrrrr. Grrrrr."

Bernard Bear tried again. This time he took an even deeper breath. "Hmmmm," he said. "Hmmmm. Hmmmm. Hmmmm."

This was no good at all. Bernard Bear took an enormous breath, so that he was full of air. He opened his mouth as wide as it would go. He clenched his paws and... "Hello!" he said. "I'm Bernard Bear!"

Poor Bernard! It didn't matter what he did or how hard he tried, he could only make the noises he had always been able to make. Of course, he could talk to other toys, but that wasn't what he wanted. He wanted to be able to sing to the children who played with him.

"You should think yourself lucky," said the toy train. "I can only whistle to humans. At least you can say a few words."

"Yes," agreed the toy duck. "If you squeeze me very hard, I sometimes squeak, but even that doesn't work if I've been left in the bath for a long time."

But Bernard just wasn't satisfied. "It's all very well," he said, "being content with what I can do already, but I'm an ambitious bear. I want to impress everyone I meet. I want people to say, 'Oh, yes, we know Bernard Bear. Isn't he amazing?' That's what I want."

"You should be careful, Bernard," said the toy train. "You might make matters worse, not better, with all your practising."

Nothing anyone could say would dissuade Bernard from pursuing his singing career. He listened hard when the children in the nursery had their singsong each afternoon. He had soon learned the words and the tunes – but he still couldn't sing the songs! So Bernard listened even harder to what the teacher had to say.

"Now children," she said. "Lift up your heads and take deep breaths. I'm going to open the window so that you can breathe in all that lovely fresh air. Then we'll sing this song as loudly as we can. Let's see if we can't wake up Bernard Bear over there and make him growl!"

"I'm not asleep, actually," muttered Bernard, but it was nice to be mentioned, all the same.

When the children had gone home that night, Bernard thought about what the teacher had said. Fresh air! That was the answer. He must fill himself up with more fresh air.

Bernard hopped over to the window and nudged it open with his paw. It slid up quite easily.

"Now, the way to get most fresh air will be to sit on the windowsill," said Bernard to himself. "Let's see. If I put one leg this side and the other leg this side, I can *just* balance."

Bernard Bear sat on the windowsill and took a deep breath. Then he took another deep breath. Then he took a third deep breath ... it was a breath too many. With a wobble and a wiggle, Bernard Bear overbalanced and fell right out of the window.

Plop! Bernard fell heavily on to a flowerbed below the window. His face was muddy. His paws were muddy. His tummy was muddy. You would hardly have recognised him as the fine bear who sat on the nursery shelf.

Next day was sunny, so the teacher took the children outside. It wasn't very long before one little boy found Bernard in the flowerbed.

The teacher took charge at once. "Let me have a look at that bear," she said. "Oh dear, he's been outside all night, I think. I'll have to take him home with me and clean him up."

That night, the teacher did her best with Bernard Bear. She rubbed him and she scrubbed him, until his fur was as clean as ever. Then she brushed him with a lovely soft brush and put him near the radiator to dry.

"Phew!" said Bernard to himself. He felt that he had had a lucky escape.

Next day, looking as bright and bonny as usual, Bernard was

taken back to the nursery. Two little girls immediately claimed him to join in their game.

"What do you say today, Bernard?" they asked, shaking him gently.

Bernard said nothing.

"Don't you want to talk to us, Bernard?" asked the little girls, poking the bear's tummy.

Bernard said nothing.

"Tell us who you are!" laughed the little girls, patting Bernard on the back.

But Bernard said not a word.

Whether it was the rubbing and the scrubbing, on the bump into the flowerbed, or simply being outside one whole night, there was no doubt about it. Bernard had lost his voice.

"If only I hadn't tried to sing," moaned Bernard to himself. "I had a lovely voice before, but now I'm just as silent as most other teddy bears. I should have been happy with who I was."

Bernard certainly had learnt his lesson, and a few days later, when one of the children gave him a little shake, he found himself making a tiny noise.

"Grrrrr," he said. "Grrrr. Grrrr."

Perhaps Bernard will get his voice back after all. I hope so, don't you?

The Beep Beep Car

Once upon a time, there was a teddy bear who had a car. Yes, he had a real car, in which he zoomed about all over the place. He visited his friends and took them for outings. He did shopping for toys who were too old or busy to go into town themselves. He even delivered cards and presents when it was Christmas time.

In fact, he was a very useful bear to know, and everything would have been fine if only he hadn't been so *noisy.* Well, it wasn't really the bear who was noisy. It was the car. *Beep! Beep! Beep! Beep!* It was terribly loud.

The teddy bear's friends never had to look out of their windows to see if he was coming. Oh no. From miles away you could hear his car beeping. There was plenty of time to have a cup of tea, and read the newspaper, *and* put your coat and hat on before he arrived at your door!

Some of the teddy's friends tried to tackle him on the rather tricky subject.

"Your car is a wonderful machine," began the ragdoll, working her way towards the important part. "But tell me, does it *have* to make such a loud beeping noise?"

"Oh yes," said the teddy bear. "That's half the fun. Why, no one would know I was coming if it wasn't for that beeping noise."

"That's very true," agreed the ragdoll, "but you know, there are times when we don't really *want* to know you are coming. I mean, the other week, for example, the poor old train jumped right off his tracks because you beeped as he was going round a corner. He did terrible damage to his axles, and he has only started to get over the shock just recently."

"Well, I'm sorry to hear that," said the teddy bear, "but really that train is going to have to pull himself together. Whoever heard of a car that didn't go *beep! beep!* sometimes? I certainly never did."

"It's not so much that it goes *beep! beep!*" the doll went on. "It's that it does it *so* loudly."

"Well, you know," replied the teddy bear, "there's not much point in a beeper you can't hear. That's what they're for, you see."

The doll couldn't think of anything else to say after that. The teddy bear had a point in a way, but she still felt that *his* car was much, much louder than any other car she had ever heard (and that included the racing cars in their shiny box, and everyone knows what a loud noise *they* make!)

One day, the teddy bear decided to take some of his friends to the seaside. They packed up some sandwiches and their swimming costumes and set off along the road to the coast.

When they reached the seaside, the teddy bear parked his car as near to the sea as he could. Further along the beach, a policeman doll waved his arms at the toys.

"You see how everyone likes my car?" said the proud teddy.

The toys went down on to the beach and were soon having so much fun that not one of them noticed a little row of waves splashing on either side of them.

After some games and some sandwiches, the toys all had a snooze in the sunshine. It was the ragdoll who woke up first, and she looked happily around.

"How lovely it is to be sitting on a little island like this," she said to herself. "Wait a minute … an island? This wasn't an island when we arrived!"

The waves were lapping on every side of the toys and the little car. Anxiously, the ragdoll woke the other toys.

"It's too deep to wade," said the teddy bear. "How are we ever going to let anyone know that we are here? There's no one in sight at all. We could drown before help comes!"

But the ragdoll smiled. "I think your car's very loud beep is about to be useful," she said.

In two minutes, the toys were all inside the car, beeping the horn for all they were worth. At least, the teddy bear beeped, and the other toys kept their hands or their paws over their ears. *Beep! Beep!*

It was not long before the toys were rescued by the waving policeman in a boat. "I did try to warn you," he said.

"What about my car?" asked the teddy bear, as they were rowed away. "I do hope the waves won't dampen its beep."

"We should be so lucky!" laughed the toys under their breath, now that they were safe and sound.

The Teddy Bears' Picnic

One day, Mrs Carolinus, who taught the smallest children at the nursery school, clapped her hands for attention and used her loudest voice.

"Children!" she called. "I have a special announcement to make, and you will each have a letter to take home to your parents. Next week we shall have a special outing to raise money for the new playground. It will be a Teddy Bears' Picnic! You can each bring your bears – but only one teddy bear each, please – and something nice to eat or drink. I'm sure we shall all have a lovely day."

The children were very excited at the news.

"My teddy bear's name is Honey," said Lauren. "He'll love coming to a picnic."

"My teddy bear has beautiful white fur and a special stripey jacket all of his own," said Carla. "He's been all over the place. I took him with me when we went overseas on holiday last year, so a little picnic won't be so exciting for *him*."

"I don't know *which* of my teddy bears to bring," said Annabelle grandly. "I've got *ten*, you know. Some of them are really too beautiful to bring outside, and others are *huge*, so I really couldn't carry them. I'll have to think about what to do."

One little girl listened to her friends talking and kept very quiet. Sally only had one teddy bear, but she loved him more than all her other toys. He was very old and rather threadbare. Two of his paws had worn out and been replaced by Sally's Mum, so he now had two blue paws and two pink paws. What Sally loved best about Rory (for that was her bear's name) was that he had been given to her by her Granny, who had moved two years earlier to live far away on the other side of the world. Sally missed her Granny terribly, but when she cuddled her old bear, she knew that her Granny loved her and was thinking about her.

"The other girls will laugh at Rory," said Sally to herself. "Poor old bear. He can't help being worn and mended."

But when Sally took the letter home to her Mum that afternoon, Mum couldn't see a problem.

"Rory is a little bit shabby because he has been loved so much," she said. "Would you want to swap him for a brand new bear?"

"Oh no," said Sally. "Never!"

The day of the picnic soon arrived. The weather was bright and sunny – just right for a lovely day out of doors. Sally's Mum had made some chocolate buns and some cheese rolls for her to take to share with the other children. She wrapped them up and put them in Sally's school bag.

"There doesn't seem to be much room in here, Sally," said her mother as she tried to tuck the food away. "Just a minute. What's this? You've put Rory in the bottom of your bag! He won't be able to see anything in there! Poor old bear!"

Sally hung her head. "I'm sorry," she said. "I was just afraid that the others would laugh at him, because he's not fluffy and new, you know."

"The only important thing is what *you* think about your teddy bear," said Mum. "If you don't laugh at him, it doesn't matter one bit what other people think. What would Granny say if she could see Rory hidden away?"

Sally knew that her mother was right. She put her bag over one shoulder and tucked Rory under the other arm.

"Come along, Rory," she said. "We've got a picnic to go to!"

Mum took Sally and Rory to the place where everyone was meeting for the picnic. It was on the outskirts of a beautiful wood. Mrs Carolinus had a list of all the children's names, and she ticked them off as they arrived.

Soon there were twenty children, all clutching their teddy bears, waiting to set off. Two other teachers had come along to help Mrs Carolinus.

"Now, before we go," called Mrs Carolinus, "I want you all to listen very carefully to what I have to say." (She was using her loudest voice again.) "It is very easy to get lost in a wood like this one," she went on, "so you must all keep up with the person in front. No dawdling! And no one, whatever happens, must stray off the path. Do you all understand?"

"Yes, we understand!" called the children.

"Then we are ready to begin," said Mrs Carolinus. "Quick march, everyone!"

The teachers and the children set off. To begin with they walked side by side, but soon the path through the trees became narrower, so they had to walk in single file. In places, bushes and brambles almost covered the path, so the teachers had to hold them out of the way as the children went past. Mrs Carolinus called out all the time to make sure that no one got lost.

"Are you there, Annabelle? All right, Sally? Keep up, Carla!"

The children had to concentrate so hard on following the person in front that there

was no time to look at other
bears or compare them. Sally
began to feel better.

"This *is* an adventure, isn't it,
Rory?" she whispered.

When they had been walking
for about half an hour, and were
deep in the forest, Mrs Carolinus
called out very loudly.

"Everybody stop!"

Unfortunately, some children
stopped more quickly than
others, so there was quite a bit
of confusion and one or two
dropped teddy bears. Soon
everyone had picked themselves
up and dusted themselves down.
Mrs Carolinus called out again.

"Now we can't stop here for our picnic because there are too many bushes and brambles," she said. "We will have to walk a little way from the path to find a clearing where we can all sit down together."

"But I thought she said we mustn't leave the path?" whispered Carla.

She knows best," said Annabelle. "After all, she *is* a teacher."

One by one, the children and teachers followed Mrs Carolinus, until they found a lovely clearing where they could spread out a cloth and all the delicious things they had brought to eat.

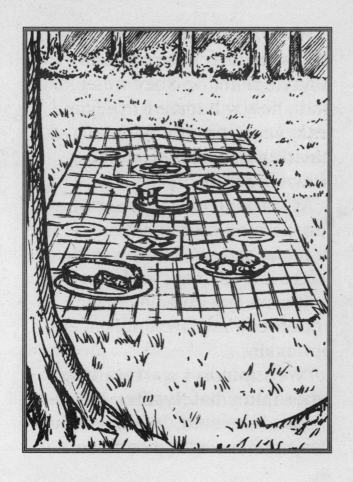

What a feast it was! And Sally didn't have to worry about anyone thinking Rory was old and shabby because everyone was much too interested in having something to eat to notice *what* her bear looked like.

At last, the children and the teachers could not eat any more. In fact, there was not very much *left* to eat! Walking in the woods had certainly given everyone an appetite. Mrs Carolinus called out again.

"We shouldn't start walking again immediately after our picnic," she said. "We must give our tummies a chance to settle.

Let's sing some songs instead.
Now, who knows any songs
about teddy bears?"

The children had a lovely time.
They sang the song about teddy
bears bouncing on the bed and
the one about the three bears.
And, of course, they sang the
song about the teddy bears'
picnic – twice!

"Now, collect up your things,"
said Mrs Carolinus, "and please
be very careful not leave
anything behind. We must leave
these beautiful woods as free of
litter as we found them. And
whatever you do, *don't* leave
your teddy bears behind!"

"As if I'd leave you, Rory," whispered Sally, as they all formed a line once more.

But for the first time, Mrs Carolinus seemed a little bit uncertain. She looked around and had a few words with the other teachers. The children saw them shaking their heads and looking a little worried. Finally, Mrs Carolinus spoke up.

"It's this way!" she called. But her voice didn't sound quite as sure as it usually did.

The children and the teachers walked for five minutes before Mrs Carolinus told everyone to stop and not to move.

"We should have reached the path by now," she said, "so I think we are slightly off course. Follow me, and we'll soon be back on track."

The children followed their teacher, whispering excitedly to each other. "Do you think we're lost?" they asked. "What are we going to do if we can't find our way home?"

Five minutes later, Mrs Carolinus called a halt again.

"This way isn't quite right either," she said. "The other teachers and I are just going to have a little talk about the best way home. Don't wander off!"

The children sat down on a nearby grassy bank. Now, for the first time, they looked at each other's bears.

"Goodness me, Sally," said Annabelle, "what a very old bear you've got there. It must be nearly an antique!"

"Yes, he's very valuable," said Sally, which wasn't strictly true, but it made her feel better, and Annabelle didn't say anything else about Rory.

After ten minutes, Carla, who had been keeping an eye on the little group of teachers, leaned forward and whispered to the others. "You know," she said, "I think we really *are* lost. I just heard Mrs Carolinus say that the best thing would be to stay where we are and wait for someone to come to look for us."

"But it will get dark!" said Annabelle. "I don't want to be in this creepy wood when it's dark!"

"Well, I don't think anyone knows the way home," said Carla, "so we don't have much choice really."

Just then, Sally heard a little whispering sound in her ear. It was Rory, trying as hard as he could to attract her attention.

"What is it, Rory?" Sally asked her old bear.

"I couldn't help overhearing what you were saying," said Rory, "and I'd like to suggest that you give the *bears* a chance to find the way home."

"Whatever do you mean?" asked Sally in surprise.

"Well," said Rory quietly, so that the other children couldn't hear, "I don't expect anyone has thought of this, but bears are used to woods and forests. That's the kind of place they come from, after all. We notice things that human beings never think about, such as whether a tree might have bark for a bear to scratch, or where there might be a hollow tree trunk to shelter in when it is cold and wet."

"So what?" hissed Sally.

"So I think I can tell the difference between one tree and the next much better than that teacher of yours," explained Rory. "But you'll have to pretend it was you who noticed, because she'll never believe me."

Sally looked long and hard at her bear. "Why don't the other bears know the way as well?" she asked slowly.

"Perhaps some of them do," said Rory. "I haven't had a chance to ask them. But, you know, most of the bears here are rather *young*. They probably haven't learnt very much about woodcraft yet."

Sally was convinced. She and Rory whispered together for a few more minutes. Then the little girl picked up her bear and made her way to where Mrs Carolinus was sitting, looking rather anxious and upset.

"Excuse me," said Sally, politely, "but I think we are really very near the path, you know. I'm quite sure we passed that tree with the silvery bark on our way here."

Mrs Carolinus looked very doubtful, but she was ready to

clutch at any straw. She sent one of the other teachers over to the silvery tree to have a look. Two minutes later, the teacher was waving excitedly. It *was* the path! They were not lost after all!

It was a tired but happy group of teachers and children who found their way to the meeting place half an hour later. The parents had begun to look at their watches, wondering what had happened to the party.

"Ah," said Mrs Carolinus quickly, "there were so many good opportunities for nature study in the woods, I'm afraid we rather lost track of time."

"We certainly lost track of something," whispered Rory, with a giggle.

That night, when Mum tucked Sally up in her bed, she asked what the other children had thought of Rory.

"They said he was old and shabby," said Sally, "but you know, I don't mind at all. There's a lot to be said for being old."

Mum couldn't help but smile at Sally's serious little face. "I'll tell Granny you said that!" she laughed, turning out the light.

The
Every-Year
Dolls

Diana picked up her last Christmas present. She had opened all the rest, and they had been full of wonderful surprises. But this present was different.

"I don't really need to open this," she said. "After all, we know exactly what's going to be inside it."

"Well, not *exactly*," her mother protested. "I do know what you mean, darling, but it is very, very kind of Granny to make a special present for you each year, especially now that her eyesight is not so good. And her fingers are not as nimble as they were, you know."

Diana did know, and she tried hard to be grateful, but it really was very hard. She couldn't help sighing as she undid the brightly coloured paper.

It had all started when Diana was three. Granny had made her a beautiful little doll, with a yellow satin skirt and a bright blue top. She had black silky hair and little red boots, and the smiliest, jolliest face you could imagine. Diana had really loved that little doll, the tiniest of the dolls she had. It was partly because she was so small and partly because Granny had made her specially – just for her.

Of course, both Diana and her
mother had told Granny how
very pleased she was with her
present. Perhaps they had said
so just one time too many, for
the next year, Granny made
another doll. It was exactly the
same as the first doll, except that
this time it had a pink skirt and a
white top and little blue boots.
Oh, and its hair was golden.

Diana quite liked having sister
dolls. They looked just right
sitting either side of the table in
her dolls' house. She told Granny
how pleased she was – and she
meant it. Granny smiled and
admired the dolls' house.

But the next year, when Diana was five, Granny made her *another* doll. It was exactly the same as the first two, but with different coloured clothes again and red hair this time. "For the dolls' house," wrote Granny on the card that came with the carefully wrapped parcel.

As the years went by, Granny became more and more frail. She could not travel to see her granddaughter any more, but she still made dolls. Each Christmas a similar parcel arrived, and each time there was a little doll inside, almost, but not exactly, like the very first one.

Diana still wrote a nice letter each year, thanking her Granny. She knew that it took the old lady longer and longer each time to make the doll, but each one was as perfect as the one before. Diana was rather old now to play with dolls, and the last thing she wanted for Christmas was *another* of the every-year dolls, as she called them, but she didn't want to hurt the old lady's feelings if she could help it.

The very last doll didn't arrive at Christmas. It was the twelfth doll, and Diana was fourteen. Granny was very ill that winter. At the end of November, a telephone call came to say that Granny had passed away peacefully in her own home. A few weeks after Christmas, Diana's mother travelled to Granny's house to sort out her things and make preparations for its sale. She found the twelfth doll, almost complete, in Granny's workbasket. Only its eyes, nose and mouth had not yet been added.

Diana's mother brought her the last doll. "I know Granny would have wanted you to have it, darling," she said.

It was many years since Diana had seen Granny. She felt a little bit sad because her mother was sad, but she did not really miss the old lady. And she certainly did not miss the every-year dolls. She put the last doll, with the others, in the box that contained some of the toys she had played with as a child, and soon forgot all about them.

Almost twenty years passed. Diana went to college and worked hard. She became a doctor and worked even harder. Then she got married and had a little girl of her own – and she worked harder still.

In all that time, Diana had not thought about her box of toys, but one day, watching her baby daughter playing with a new plastic doll, she suddenly thought of the box tucked away in the attic. When the baby was in bed, she found the box and brought it downstairs.

As she opened the box, Diana felt the years slip away. One by one, she took out the little dolls, but now she looked at them with different eyes. She noticed for the first time how beautifully they were made. The stitches were tiny. The fabrics were soft and in lovely colours. Best of all were the tiny faces, each with its own laughing expression. For the first time in years, Diana thought of her Granny and all the patience and love that had gone into each tiny doll. Tears came to her eyes.

It was almost Christmas again, and Diana could not bear to put the dolls away again. Her own little girl was much too small to play with them – they were so perfect and fragile.

Diana picked up the dolls one by one and put them side by side along the mantelpiece. Their outstretched arms touched each other, as though the twelve little dolls were holding hands. They looked lovely.

As Diana stood and looked at the dolls, her husband came into the room. Glancing at the mantelpiece he said, "Oh, you've started putting the Christmas decorations up. How lovely!"

Diana smiled. It was only a few weeks before Christmas. Now she knew exactly what to do with the little dolls.

That evening, Diana carefully sewed the dolls together, so that one little hand clasped the next. Last of all, she found some embroidery thread and gently put two eyes, a little nose, and a mouth on the last little doll. She took a long time over it, for she wanted it to be just as fine as the other dolls. Then she pinned up the string of dolls above the mantelpiece, where they looked as bright and colourful as any Christmas decoration.

As Diana's baby grew older, she noticed that the dolls were put in the same place each Christmas.

"They're so pretty," she said. "Where did they come from?"

So Diana told her the story of the twelve little dolls.

"And will we have them *every* year?" asked the little girl.

"Of course," said Diana. "They are every-year dolls – and always will be."

The
Surprise
Box

Once there was an annoying little boy who had a habit of guessing what was in the presents he was given each year for his birthday. You can imagine what it was like. A kindly aunt would come to visit, holding a present with bright wrapping paper and a ribbon tied in a great big bow.

"Happy birthday, Robert," she would say. "I hope you like this."

Robert would take the present, shake it, prod it, pass it from hand to hand and, without undoing it, say, "Oh, it feels like socks. Thank you very much, Aunty Joy."

"Well, yes, it is," Aunty Joy would say, looking disappointed. "Aren't you going to open them?"

"All right," Robert would reply, "but it's not so much fun when it's not a surprise."

Now this was hardly fair. No one forced Robert to guess what was in his parcels. It was just a pity he seemed to guess so well. In fact, Robert was very lucky, after a while, that his friends and relations *gave* him presents. It wasn't much fun seeing him open them, after all.

One year, Robert's Uncle Paul decided to teach him a lesson. He came to visit on Robert's birthday as usual and put a large box on the table in front of his only nephew.

Robert picked up the box. He shook it. He turned it round. He prodded it. He lifted it up and down. He even sniffed at it! He had to confess that he hadn't a clue what was inside.

"Well, open it," said Uncle Paul.

Robert felt rather more interested in this present than in some of the others he had been given. He undid the ribbon and carefully took off the paper. Inside … was another parcel!

"Now you can guess, I expect," said Uncle Paul.

Once again, Robert went through his shaking, prodding, sniffing routine. He still couldn't tell what was in the parcel.

"So open it," smiled his uncle.

Paul undid the next ribbon. He took off another layer of wrapping paper to find ... yes, you've guessed, yet *another* colourful present inside.

"Can't you guess yet?" teased Uncle Paul.

Robert scowled. He did everything he could think of to the parcel and wished he had an X-ray machine. He still couldn't work out what was inside.

"Open it!" laughed Uncle Paul.

Once again, Robert undid the wrapping paper – only to find another colourful layer inside.

"I don't think there's anything inside here," said Robert. "It's just layer after layer of paper."

"Oh no, it isn't!" said Uncle Paul. "There's quite definitely a present in there, but I'm amazed that you can't work out what it is. You're usually so clever."

That made Robert even more cross. He tore off more and more and more paper, until at last he came to a brightly painted wooden box.

"*Now* what do you think it is?" asked his uncle.

Robert shook the box. There was no sound. He tapped it. It didn't sound hollow or full, just ordinary. He sniffed it. It didn't smell of anything except wood.

"Well?" asked Uncle Paul. "What is it?"

Robert had to smile. "I don't have a clue," he said. "It's the first present I haven't been able to guess for *ages*." Then he grinned more broadly. "I suppose," he said, "there is one thing I can say that it definitely *is* … it's a surprise!"

And it was! Turn the page to find out what Robert saw when he opened the box!

Woah! Rocking Horse!

What do you do with a rocking horse who is wild? One who bucks and gallops and generally acts as though he is out on the open plains, free to do as he likes? The rocking horse at the Tiny Tots Playgroup was just like that.

In fact, it wasn't really that the rocking horse was nasty and vicious. He didn't mean to send so many little children tumbling from his back when he put on a spurt of speed or kicked up his legs. It was just that the children, very often, were excited to be sitting on the beautiful rocking horse. They grabbed his mane in their plump little hands and kicked their strong little legs into his sides. Well, any horse will get excited as well, if he is treated like that. Sometimes the children shrieked with joy as the horse began to move, and that just made him worse. What with the kicking and the tugging and the shrieking, the rocking horse would leap into action. He would begin to move faster and faster, rearing and rocking higher and higher, until the children screamed with fright instead of excitement and several of them, as I said before, fell right off on to the carpet.

Luckily, no one was hurt by the wild rocking horse, but most of the children were badly frightened, and they certainly didn't want to sit on the rocking horse again. They didn't understand that if *they* were gentle with the rocking horse, he would be gentle with them.

It was not surprising that the rocking horse soon had a very bad reputation. "Don't go near that horse," the playgroup leader would tell the children. "It's not safe at all."

With no one to ride him, the rocking horse became very sad. Unfortunately, when a brave child did jump on his back, the rocking horse was so surprised and pleased that he kicked up his heels more than ever. It really was a vicious circle.

Then, one day, a new little girl came to the playgroup. She had been in hospital for a long time and was still very frail and pale. Although she was nearly four, she couldn't walk very well, and had to be lifted in and out of her chair to sit on the floor at story-time or join the other children singing nursery rhymes.

The little girl did not seem to be interested in anything very much. She had spent so much time by herself that she had forgotten how to play with other children. In any case, she felt so ill and tired a lot of the time that nothing interested her much.

But when the little girl, whose name was Tina, had been at the playgroup for a couple of days, she noticed the rocking horse in the corner.

"I want to ride on *that*," she said. It was the longest sentence that anyone had heard her say.

"I don't think so, Tina," said the playgroup leader. "That horse isn't very safe, and you are not very strong yet. Wait until you are feeling better."

But Tina didn't want to wait. She felt as if she had spent all her life waiting – waiting to go into hospital, waiting for an operation, waiting to feel better, waiting to run around like other children of her age.

Day after day, the little girl made the same request, and at last the playgroup leader agreed. After all, nothing else seemed to interest Tina

The playgroup leader cleared a big space on the floor. She put down a lot of cushions, in case of accidents, and stood nearby to catch the little girl when she fell – as she was sure she would.

But when Tina sat on the horse's back, she didn't pull his mane or kick her feet. She sat quietly and held the reins, feeling the horse beginning to move, ever so slowly.

The playgroup leader was amazed. Gradually, she began to relax and moved away from the horse, for he was behaving beautifully. No pony ever trotted so gently with a little girl on his back. The horse went slowly, slowly for half an hour, getting to know his rider, until Tina became tired and asked to be lifted down.

After that, Tina rode the big rocking horse every day. And

very, very gradually, the horse began to speed up. As Tina grew stronger, she was able to sit up straighter and hold the reins more tightly. Her eyes began to sparkle and a faint pink colour came to her cheeks. She began to take an interest in other things that were happening at the playgroup, too. Every day she grew happier and healthier.

On the last day of term, Tina's parents came to take her home from playgroup. They were very pleased with the way she had been improving, but they had never seen her ride the rocking horse, and they did not know why her eyes were brighter and her smiles were broader.

The playgroup leader greeted Tina's parents as they came into the big room. In the corner, a little girl was riding the rocking horse, higher and higher, and faster and faster, her hair flying out behind her as she rode.

"Ah," sighed Tina's mother, "how I hope the day will come when our little girl can do that. It has been such a struggle for her, though she *is* so much better now."

The teacher laughed. "That *is* your little girl," she said "And she's as wild as the rocking horse – I'm very happy to say!"

The
Real Baby
Doll

One day, Beatrice's mother gave her a present. This was strange, because it wasn't Christmas, or her birthday, or a special day of any kind. Inside the wrapping paper was a baby doll, wearing a little white stretchy suit and with its own shawl and bottle of milk.

"I don't like dolls," said Beatrice. "And I specially don't like baby dolls. They don't *do* anything."

Beatrice's mother sighed. "Well, no, they don't do anything much at first," she said, "except sleep and drink their milk, but they need *you* to do something. They need you to love them and look after them. I think you could do that, Bea, couldn't you?"

"Why should I?" asked Beatrice. "I like toys that move or play tunes or light up or something. Not like this silly doll."

The little girl's mother tried again. "The reason I thought you might like a baby doll to look after," she said, "is that I'm going to be having a baby soon – a little sister for you, Bea – and I thought it would be fun if we could both look after our babies together."

But Beatrice looked at her Mum with a big scowl on her face. "You can take this doll back," she said, "and you can take *your* baby back, too. We're quite happy as we are, aren't we? We don't need one of those silly babies here. Don't let's talk about it any more. Promise?"

"I can't take either of the babies back, Bea," said her mother gently. "Perhaps you'll change your mind in a little while."

But Beatrice continued to show no interest at all in the baby doll. Her mother showed her how to wash it and feed it and cuddle it. But Bea was always impatient to get back to her other toys. She hid the doll in a cupboard, but somehow her mother always found it and brought it out again.

A few weeks later, Beatrice's father came into her room late one night. "Aunty Julia has come to look after you tonight, Bea," he said, "because I'm going with Mummy to get our new baby. Isn't it exciting?"

"Well, I hope you're not going to bring it back *here*," said Beatrice. "I told Mummy we don't need it."

But in the morning, Daddy came back and carried Beatrice into the sitting room. Mummy was propped up on the sofa, and in her arms she held a little pink and white bundle.

"Come and see our baby, Bea," she said, and she looked rather anxiously at her little girl.

Beatrice came forward and put out her hand. She touched the baby's soft little hand and cried out in amazement. "But she's *warm*! She's not like a doll at all!"

And the baby, hearing her sister's voice, closed her little fingers around Beatrice's thumb.

"Oh, Mum," breathed Beatrice, "I've got such a good idea. You can have *my* baby doll, and I'll have this one. She's much, much nicer." And she bent down to kiss the little head.

"Let's share her," said her mother. "This little one belongs to *all* of us."

Della
Duck's
Adventure

When Amy was a baby, her big brother gave her a yellow duck to play with in her bath. Amy loved playing with it from the start. She tried to drown it every night, but the little duck always came bobbing up to the surface again, as large as life.

A few weeks later, Amy tried to get rid of the duck in another way. Over and over again, she threw it as far as she could with her chubby little arms. She got so good at throwing that the duck often hit the bathroom wall and bounced back again, sometimes falling with a *plop!*

right back into the bath. Night
after night, Amy's mother, or her
father, or her big brother
patiently picked up the duck and
put it back in the water.

As Amy got bigger, the duck
had lots more attacks to suffer.
One summer's day, Amy threw it
right out of the bathroom
window, which was open a tiny
bit at the top.

"That child should play basket-
ball," said her father, admiring
the little girl's aim. As the family
lived on the sixth floor of a block
of flats, Amy's big brother had to
hurry down several flights of
stairs to find the little duck out

in the car park. After that, Amy's parents kept the bathroom window shut *all* the time.

I'm afraid Amy's next game with the duck was even worse. She (this is quite embarrassing) tried to flush him down the lavatory! Amy was not very pleased when the little duck came bobbing up again, and Amy's mother was not very pleased either at having to fish out the duck and take it away for a thorough cleaning and disinfecting before Amy could have it back again.

Not surprisingly, Amy didn't want to play with the duck for a while, but as the years went by, she found that the little yellow bird was extremely useful in lots of different games. It made a wonderful target. As Amy grew up, the duck had bean bags, pingpong balls, arrows and even pretend grenades thrown at it.

Later on, Amy used the duck for lots of different experiments. She took it to school and catapulted it across the playground and into a nearby field to show how levers work. She took it to summer camp and let it float right out into the middle of a lake to practise her life-saving skills. She took it to the park and perched it on the edge of a pond to see how real ducks would react to it (they either ignored it or pecked it).

After all that, you might have thought that the duck would be rather scratched and bashed, but it actually looked as fresh and bright as the day it was made. With its yellow body and orange beak, the duck looked as good as new.

During all those years, the duck was given many names. Amy's father called it "The Indestructible Duck". Amy's big brother called it "The Unthinkable Unsinkable", but Amy one day named her duck after one of her teachers, who had a voice rather like a quack! After that, it was always Della Duck.

You might think that Della Duck had already had enough adventures to last a liftetime, but Amy had not finished with her yet. In her last year at school, Amy took part in a balloon race. You probably know all about them. Hundreds of people write their names and addresses on labels hanging from balloons. Then the balloons are released and float far away. When the balloons finally come to rest, sometimes months later, anyone who finds them can post off the label, saying where the balloon was found. The person whose balloon is found to have travelled the farthest is the winner.

It would be silly, really, to attach anything else to the balloon, because it would weigh the balloon down and stop it travelling so far, but one or two members of Amy's class started adding little things to their balloons, and the craze spread. Some people tied on a tiny teddy bear or a photograph of themselves.I don't suppose I need to tell you what Amy decided to tie on to her balloon.

At last the day came when all the balloons were released. Up they went, pink, purple, blue, yellow and green – and one of them had a very brave little duck attached to it!

After a few days, some of the labels from the balloons began to arrive. They had been found many miles away. After a few weeks, even more labels had been returned, and some of them came from hundreds of miles away. But as the weeks turned into months, there was no news of Amy's balloon, or of her old friend Della Duck.

"The balloon might have landed in the middle of a forest or in a desert," said Amy's brother. "No one will ever find it there. Or it might have come down over the sea."

"Well, that would be all right," retorted Amy. "We all know that Della can float. In fact, that duck is impossible to sink."

"True enough," said her brother, "but that doesn't mean that anyone would *find* her.

There's an awful lot of ocean out there, after all."

Even several months after the balloon competition, labels were still arriving, even though the finishing date had passed. A very few balloons had travelled right across the sea and reached other countries. Some of the balloon-senders began writing to the people who had returned the labels, for they felt as if they were special penfriends.

But there was no news of Della. Finally, Amy had to admit that it was very unlikely that the duck would now be found. It could be anywhere in the world by now.

"You're right," Amy told her big brother. "That duck could have fallen in a quarry or a jungle. I just wish I knew where Della was, that's all. I'd just like to *know*."

"Well, you played with that duck longer than I ever thought you would," laughed her brother. "It's the most successful present I've ever given you."

On Amy's next birthday, her brother gave her a tiny box. "I thought we should mark a sad occasion," he smiled. "I hope you like them."

Inside the box was a pair of tiny earrings – shaped like ducks!

"Now I'll never forget Della," laughed Amy, "wherever she is!"

It was not long before Amy left school. She had been wondering for a long time what kind of job she might like to do. Somehow, thinking about Della and where she might be in the world made Amy feel that she too would like to travel – not attached to a balloon, perhaps! Amy was lucky to find a job quite soon that was just what she wanted. She worked for a travel agency, and after a year or so began to travel all over the world, seeing many of the places that she had only dreamed of before.

Amy loved her job, especially as she sometimes was able to stay a few extra days in the places she visited, so that she could have a little holiday of her own. It was when she was lying on a beautiful, sunny beach on the island of Hawaii that the most extraordinary thing happened.

Amy was feeling hot and went down to the edge of the sea for a cooling swim. But as she came to the edge of the water, Amy kicked something in the sand. She thought it was a shell or a pebble and almost didn't bother to look down, but something made her kneel down on the warm sand and take a look. A little orange beak was poking out of the sand!

"Della!" cried Amy, brushing away the rest of the sand. It certainly was a little yellow duck, and it *looked* just like Della, but whether it really was that famous duck I couldn't say.

Amy wrapped the duck up carefully and sent it to her brother, who now had a little boy of his own. "For Toby," she wrote on the label, "hoping Della has even more adventures with you."

Well, she did, you know, but that is quite another story and for another time...

Titles in this Series include